THE
INNKEEPER'S
DAUGHTER

BY JILL BRISCOE

ILLUSTRATED BY DENNIS HOCKERMAN

To my daughter-in-law Debbie,
whom I love very much

Ideals Publishing Corporation
Milwaukee, Wisconsin

ISBN 0-8249-8073-5

Keturah was unhappy, so she ran to the stable where she usually went when things went wrong. She loved the animals who were kept there, especially Donkey. He was her favorite. He always seemed to understand when nobody else did. He never yelled at her or told her she was stupid. He was gentle and sweet and rubbed his soft nose in her hair when she was upset. She always felt better when she'd had a talk with Donkey about her worries.

Keturah had needed a place to run to ever since she discovered she was different from other children. It was really very, very sad, but Keturah had crippled hands. The boys and girls in her street were cruel to her. She felt awful when a ball was thrown to her and she couldn't catch it or when a kitten needed petting and she couldn't pick it up.

Keturah found her way into the darkest corner of the stable where Donkey was kept. He recognized Keturah at once and seemed to smile. All the animals knew the little girl and they all loved her. She never played rough tricks on them or poked them with sharp sticks like some of the children in the village.

That night the stable was more crowded than usual. Keturah couldn't remember when the village had been so busy. Her father had told her that the Romans, who ruled her town of Bethlehem, had ordered everyone to return to the city of his birth so they could take a census. "What's a census, Father?" Keturah had asked, but the question was brushed aside. Keturah's father was a busy man and had no time for a little girl's questions. "If only you had proper hands, you could help us," he said impatiently; and then he was sorry.

He sighed as Keturah, in tears, spun around and ran out of the inn toward the stable. Keturah's father was a good man at heart and didn't mean to be unkind. But today he was tired with all the work the census was causing him. He had been bitterly disappointed when his little girl had been born without proper fingers. "What will become of her?" he wondered sadly. Who would want to marry a girl with crippled hands? His thoughts were rudely interrupted by some noisy visitors from Judea. After giving their animals to the stable boy, the innkeeper made his way back to the inn.

Keturah sat quietly in Donkey's stall. She brushed the animal's side with her nose, wishing she could tickle him with her fingers. One of his hooves was bent. She knew he understood just how she felt. She wondered why God had given fingers to all of her friends but had not given them to her. She knew it could not have been because she was naughty, because God didn't punish people like that. It wouldn't be right and God always did what was right. Keturah sighed and tried not to think about it any more.

The visitors kept coming and soon the stable could not hold any more animals. The horses were pushing and shoving each other to get to the hay. The ox, who lived in the stable in the cold weather, was very cross because now he had to share his stall with a proud stallion who had carried his fancy master all the way from Jericho.

Keturah leaned her head against Donkey's side and big tears flowed down her cheek. She was thinking about her father and mother and how she longed to help them keep the inn tidy. Her mother was always baking bread or arranging flowers for the guest rooms. Keturah loved her parents so very much. It made her unhappy when she couldn't play her part.

Suddenly there was a loud voice at the stable door. A rough-looking man and an equally rough-looking donkey were standing at the entrance. The man tried to push his animal inside the door. But the stable boy protested, saying it wasn't fair to the other animals. At that, the rough visitor began beating the stable boy with a stick, sending him running home with a bruised face. The rough donkey pushed its way toward Keturah and she shrank back into the shadows, wondering if she would ever be able to get out of the stable.

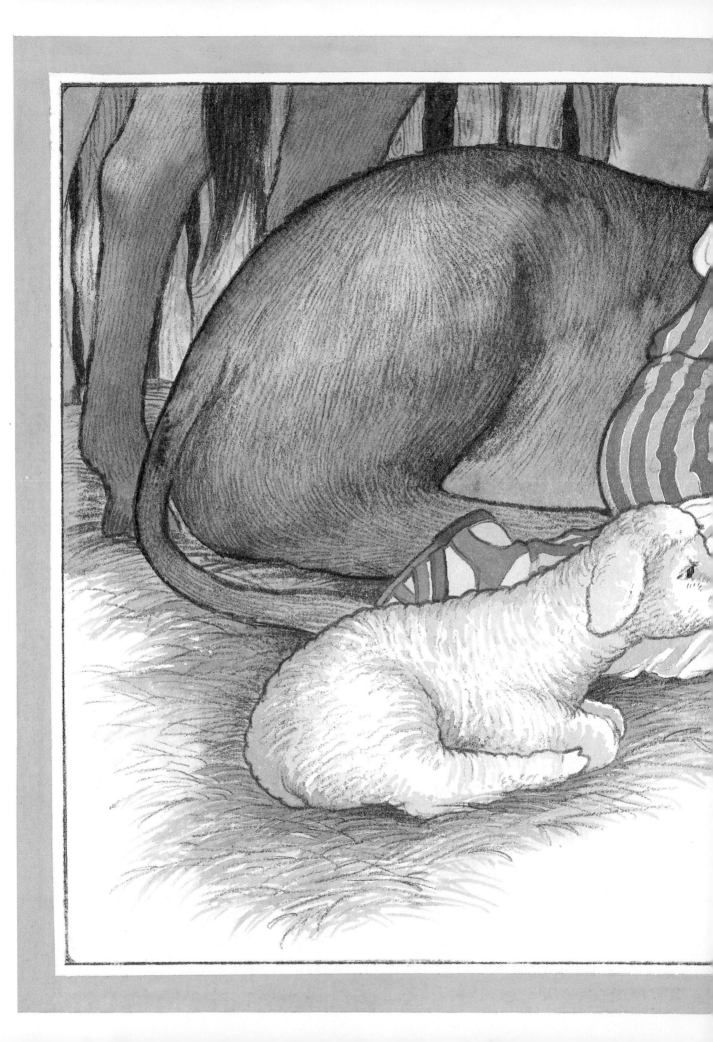

After trying to squeeze past the rough donkey and the proud stallion, Keturah gave up and returned to Donkey's side. No one would care if she just stayed here for the night. Her parents were far too busy to notice she wasn't in bed. She could still hear people arriving at the inn, so she snuggled up to Donkey, who cradled her head on his soft side and seemed to tell her to go to sleep.

Keturah began to have the strangest dream; at least she thought it was a dream. She saw a blinding light and looked around to see where it was coming from. There was a slit in the roof just above the doorway, and Keturah realized the light was coming through that. Looking up through it she saw the most beautiful star she had ever seen in her life. It was all the colors of a rainbow, mixed with the soft hues of heaven, and she was quite sure it was smiling! She didn't know that stars smiled. She had never seen a star so bright or with such an odd shape. It had one long finger that was pointing right down to the stable!

Keturah couldn't squeeze around the rough donkey and the proud stallion to go outside for a better look at the star.

Suddenly the bright light made the stable look as bright as day, and Keturah could not believe what she was seeing.

"This must be a dream, but the strangest one I've ever had," she said to herself. The stable was full of children. "Where have they all come from?" Keturah wondered. She had never seen such children as these! She didn't recognize one of them and was quite sure they didn't live in the village. They were small and chubby and had funny arms sticking out of their shoulders. Their arms looked like — well, like wings! The children had long sleeves on their robes, and Keturah couldn't see if they had arms like hers as well as wings. Keturah felt good about that. If the children had funny arms, they wouldn't be unkind to a little girl with funny hands, she thought!

One of the chubby cherubs (for that was indeed what they were) was trying to comb the dust out of Donkey's tail. The small angel had a dirty face and a black stain right down his beautiful, white clothes.

"Oh dear," he puffed. "I'm not used to doing this. We don't have donkeys at home!"

"Where's home?" asked Keturah shyly, but the cherub didn't answer, even though he glanced at her with a mischievous twinkle.

Donkey loved it! He was lying in the stall with the biggest grin Keturah had ever seen on his face, as if to say "please don't stop." Keturah peeped around Donkey's stall and saw that all the other animals had been groomed as well, and even the shaggy donkey had had a bath. The two little cherubs in charge of him were wet and bedraggled, but they were giggling about it all and were trying to get the rough, old animal to smile. They tweaked his tail and tied his ears into funny knots, but they couldn't get him to do anything more than grunt.

"Poor beast," said one cherub to the other. "He's been mistreated for so long he's forgotten what it's like to smile!"

"They're coming soon," one of the cherubs whispered in Donkey's ear. He seemed to understand and shuffled his hooves excitedly as if he was doing a little dance.

"Who's coming soon?" Keturah asked Donkey,

overhearing the words. But Donkey didn't answer.

Suddenly there was a huge commotion at the stable door. Three huge camels loomed in the opening. Keturah had never seen camels at such close quarters before. They looked very haughty and were dressed up as if they belonged to very important people.

"I hope they're not going to try to come in here as well," Keturah whispered to Donkey. But the camels were tied up in the courtyard and left there. Looking around the stable, Keturah was shocked to find the cherubs had all disappeared as swiftly as they had come. She jumped as one came whizzing back at a terrific rate with some scented herbs in his hand which he scattered furiously in every direction to sweeten the air. "It is a bit smelly," mused Keturah, but with so many animals in such close quarters, the herbs didn't seem to help!

Keturah climbed on top of Donkey to see if she could get a better view of the star. Looking through the crack in the roof, she saw her father coming towards the stable and she quickly jumped off Donkey's back and hid, trembling, in the straw. Maybe she would get a beating because she was not in bed, she thought.

But Keturah's father was not thinking about her. He had not even bothered to find out that she was missing from her room. He had his own worries. His inn was full and even his stable was bulging at the seams; but he had to find room for two more people. One of them was a young girl who couldn't have been more than fifteen years of age, who was about to have a baby! "What a time to choose," he thought grimly. There wasn't one single space left in the inn, and his wife was far too busy to help the young lady. Her husband looked as though he couldn't afford to pay for his food even if a spot could be found!

Glancing inside the stable, Keturah's father turned
to the young maiden's husband and said, "There's
room in that corner stall with the donkey if you like.
There's nowhere else." The man began to protest, but
the young maid stopped him.

"Joseph, this will do," she said wearily but
thankfully. "It's warm and it's better than the field!"

Keturah's father disappeared, and the man and his
maid pushed their way into the stable and out of the
chill wind that had sprung up. Keturah was frightened.

Now she would be found and she would get a whipping
after all.

The young woman, whose name was Mary, saw
her first. She was startled but quickly recovered and,
turning to her husband, said, "Why, Joseph, look!
Here is a little maid in the stall with the sweet donkey.
The animal looks just like our gentle beast, and the
little girl has lovely eyes!"

"Hello," Joseph said, in a nice, deep, comfortable
sort of voice that made Keturah feel safe at once.

Keturah gazed into Mary's face and smiled a swift grateful smile. Then she asked, "May I stay here? I promise to be very, very quiet."

Mary nodded yes. Then she bent over and called to the man, "Joseph, hurry, the baby is coming!"

Keturah gasped. The maid was going to have her baby right here and now! Keturah knew her mother was far too busy to come and help her. Whatever would they do?

"I'll go and get some help from the inn," Joseph said, hurrying out the door. Keturah looked anxiously at the maid. She felt so helpless that she hid her hands in the folds of her wide robe. The gentle maid thanked Keturah for sharing her bed with her.

Keturah felt her heart beating with fear. The baby was about to be born and she was going to be there when it happened! What would she do if the man asked her to pour the water, or stroke the maid's hair, or *hold the baby*?

All through the night the animals in the stables were as still as they could be. But out in the courtyard, the camels seemed to be showing the horses how to kneel. Keturah thought she heard them talking, saying something about having to kneel down when the King came. "Which king?" wondered Keturah. "I must be dreaming," she said out loud.

The bright star brilliantly lit up everything. Keturah helped Joseph clean out the manger and helped put fresh hay in it. Joseph was very pleased with Keturah's idea of using the manger for a crib and kept saying, "Thank you, Keturah." Very few people ever called her by her name. They used cruel nicknames to remind her of her handicap. Few people ever said thank you to her. The little girl was beside herself with joy.

She opened her eyes to find Mary bathing her face! "Poor little girl," she was saying. "Don't be afraid. Come and look at Jesus."

"Jesus?" stammered Keturah, "Is that what you're calling Him?"

"Yes," the maid replied. "He's a very special baby. Before He was conceived, God sent His angel Gabriel to tell me what His name was to be. Jesus has been sent into the world to save His people from their sins."

Suddenly some shepherds appeared in the doorway. They

pushed their way past the rough donkey to Mary. When they saw
the baby wrapped in strips of cloth, they fell on their knees and
bowed their heads before Him. Keturah knew these shepherds. They
were not in the habit of worshiping anyone! Why, they hardly ever
went to the synagogue! "What babe is this?" wondered Keturah.
"What king lies in the manger bed, that He should have His own
special star marking the place of His birth, and angels hovering
above His bed?" She listened in amazement as the shepherds told
Joseph and Mary their story.

"Angels from heaven came to our hillside as we were keeping watch over our flock," they said. "They told us that Christ had been born in Bethlehem, for us! A Savior! Emmanuel! We came with haste to see if these things were so."

Keturah began to understand a lot of things. She knew the cherubs she thought she had dreamed about had been real. She understood why the bright star was pointing its heavenly finger at the stable, and why the camels were behaving in such a strange way! God was visiting His people! For the first time in her life, Keturah thanked God for her crippled hands. She suddenly realized she didn't care about her withered fingers anymore.

"Why, just think," she said to herself. "If I had had proper hands I wouldn't even have been here tonight! I wouldn't have seen Jesus!" Creeping around Donkey, Keturah fell on her knees beside the shepherds. She couldn't quite see because her eyes were full of tears. When at last she looked up, the shepherds had gone back to their flocks. In their place knelt three of the most richly dressed men Keturah had ever seen.

"Are you angels too?" she asked in astonishment. But the men weren't listening to Keturah, they were talking excitedly with Joseph and laying down gifts beside the manger bed. There were jars of sweet frankincense and myrrh and a small chest of gold. Joseph asked one of the kings, "Where have you come from?"

The man replied, "We have seen His star in the east and have come to worship Him."

Keturah couldn't help but interrupt the man and ask her own question. "Is the star you saw in the east the same one that hangs over our stable?"

The man answered her kindly, saying, "Yes, young maid. The star is very important to us. It tells us that a king is born!"

After the men from the east had gone to rest at the inn, Keturah lay down beside Donkey thinking how amazing it all was. She couldn't help being a little angry at her father who left the man and his maid and the newborn baby in the stable while taking the wealthy and wise men from the east into his inn. Hadn't he told Mary and Joseph it was full? It didn't seem right that they had beds, while the baby they had come to worship slept in a cattle stall and His parents rested on beds of hay!

But Keturah couldn't be angry for very long. She was too happy. After all, she told herself, her father had not realized how important his visitors were and at least he had not turned them away.

Keturah's thoughts were interrupted by Mary's voice.

"Keturah, come here," she said. Keturah scrambled off her bed of hay and appeared at Mary's side in an instant.

"Keturah, would you like to hold the baby?" asked Mary gently. Keturah nearly fainted away for the second time that night.

"Hold the baby!" she gasped. "Oh yes, I'd love to!" But then a great horror swept over her. In all the excitement she had forgotten her withered hands! Mary didn't know she didn't have any fingers. She couldn't hold the baby. She might drop Him. A great sob shook the little girl's frame, and she scampered back to the dark corner of Donkey's stall and flung

herself down on the floor, crying her heart out.

Almost immediately she felt Mary's soft hand on her shoulder. The young mother had come to her at once, and was comforting her as best as she could.

"Keturah, don't cry. Whatever is the matter?" But Keturah couldn't tell her.

"Keturah, I know about your hands," Mary said quietly. "Is that what is bothering you?"

"You know?" gasped Keturah, in amazement, choking back her tears.

"I saw them when you helped Joseph make the manger bed," Mary said simply. "It doesn't matter, Keturah. I still want you to hold the baby if you'd like to." Keturah couldn't believe her ears. Mary still wanted her to hold Jesus!

Mary went back to the rough trough that was serving as a crib and lifted the little Lord Jesus out of it. Then she came back to Keturah who was sitting on the floor, her eyes every bit as bright and shining as the huge star that shone over the stable door.

"Does He know about my hands?" Keturah whispered to Mary as she stretched out her arms for the bundle of life.

"I'm sure He knows. He doesn't mind," replied Mary smiling. Placing Jesus in Keturah's arms, Mary returned to Joseph, tired beyond measure. "Put Him back in the manger when you're ready," she said to the little girl as she fell asleep.

Keturah didn't know how long she held the Christ. How do you count the moments when God is in your arms? She had never in her life felt as she felt then. Her heart was pounding with excitement. Her body tingled with warmth and happiness. Her very soul seemed to be on fire with love and thankfulness. Tears of joy rolled down her cheeks, splashing onto the baby Jesus's sleeping face, and she hastened to wipe them away.